W9-BTF-758

Things That Fly

Published by Advance Publishers, L.C.
www.advance-publishers.com

Written by Ronald Kidd
Art layout by J.J. Smith-Moore
Art composition by sheena needham • ess design
Produced by Bumpy Slide Books

ISBN: 1-57973-073-6

Blue's Clues Discovery Series

Hi! It's me, Steve. My puppy Blue is inside right now, making something. She didn't want me to see what it is, because it's a secret. Should I knock on the door to find out how she's doing? Okay!

Blue, our friends are here. Are you finished? Great! Let's go on in!

Wow! That's a pretty big box, Blue! Is what you made inside? Hmmm . . . I wonder what it is. Could you give us a hint about what you made? Ah . . . it's something for show-and-tell at school. Oh, and the theme of show-and-tell is stuff that floats or flies in the air? So what are you bringing, Blue?

Oh, good idea! You want us to play Blue's Clues to figure out what you made for show-and-tell! I love Blue's Clues!

Do you want to play, too? You do? Great! Let's go!

Well, here we are at school. And here are all of Blue's friends! I wonder why everyone is outside. Oh, right! Blue's class is having show-and-tell outside because everyone is bringing something that floats or flies in the air.

Do you see a clue? Oh, here it is. It's one of the tails on the wind sock. Our first clue is a tail! Hmmm . . . what do you think Blue made that has a tail and flies or floats in the air? I think we need to find two more clues before we can figure out what Blue has made for show-and-tell.

Wow! Look at all of the things that are floating or flying in the air! Should we look around and see how many we can find? Great!

Hey! Show-and-tell is starting. What is Purple Kangaroo holding? Yeah! A balloon! Right! A balloon floats in the air. Cool!

You see a clue? Oh yeah, the string on the balloon. That's our second clue!

So what could Blue have made for show-and-tell that has a tail and a string? Do you know? Maybe we should keep looking for our last clue.

Orange Kitten brought a sheet of paper for show-and-tell. But a sheet of paper doesn't fly, does it. I wonder what she's going to do with that? Oh, look. She's folding the paper up. What do you think she's making?

Yeah! A paper airplane! Cool. A paper airplane flies in the air. And there it goes!

Uh-oh. Green Puppy forgot to bring something for show-and-tell. Maybe we can help her find something that floats or flies in the air.

Good job! Over there, Green Puppy! It's a feather! Now Green Puppy has something to share, too!

Magenta is up next! She's
brought a ball for show-and-tell.
Do balls fly through the air? Oh, good
thinking! Balls fly when you throw them.

You see a clue? Oh, the diamond shape! Hey! We have all three clues! Let's try to figure out what Blue has made for show-and-tell.

Okay, our three clues are a tail, a string, and a diamond shape. When you put them together, they make something that floats or flies in the air. Hmmm . . . that's a hard one. Do you know what it could be?

A kite! Blue made a kite for show-and-tell!
We just figured out Blue's Clues! You are so smart!
Hey! Blue made her own kite, so maybe she
could help us make one, too. That sounds
great! Thanks for coming to show-and-tell!

BLUE'S FLYING KITE

You will need: scissors, glue, tape, ball of string, a pencil, crepe paper streamer, 2 lightweight sticks, and a newspaper or large sheet of drawing paper

1. Ask an adult to cut
V-shaped notches in stick ends.

2. Place sticks in the shape of a
cross to form the frame for the kite.

3. Crisscross string around where
the sticks join; coat string with glue.

4. Run another piece of string through notches and
around outside of frame; tie ends to make string tight.

5. Place frame on paper and trace the shape, but
make the tracing a little bigger than the real frame.
Cut out your tracing.

6. Fold paper edges over string of frame and glue down.

7. Run a piece of string along the short stick, feeding
it through the notches and tying it in front of the kite.
Have an adult snip the ends of the string. Repeat, running
a piece of string along the long stick and tying it in front.

8. Take the end of a ball of string and tie at
the point where the short and long strings cross.

9. Cut crepe paper streamer to 1-1/2 times height
of frame; tie to bottom of frame to form tail. Go fly a kite!